# Good Night, Hattie, My Dearie, My Dove

# Good Night, Hattie,

# My Dearie, My Dove

by
## Alice Schertle

illustrated by
## Ted Rand

**H**arperCollins*Publishers*

1 2 3 4 5 6 7 8 9 10

Good Night, Hattie, My Dearie, My Dove
Text copyright © 1985, 2002 by Alice Schertle
Illustrations copyright © 2002 by Ted Rand
Printed in Singapore. All rights reserved.
www.harperchildrens.com

Library of Congress Cataloging-in-Publication Data   Schertle, Alice.
Good night, Hattie, my dearie, my dove / by Alice Schertle / illustrated by Ted Rand.   p.     cm.
Summary: After following her nine toys in a parade through the house, Hattie explains why each of them
needs to sleep with her in her bed.   ISBN 0-688-16022-0 — ISBN 0-688-16023-9 (lib. bdg.)
[1. Bedtime—Fiction.   2. Counting.   3. Toys—Fiction.]   I. Title: Good night, Hattie, my dearie, my dove.
II. Rand, Ted, ill.   III. Title.   PZ7.S3442 Gn   2002   00-054111   [E]—dc21   CIP   AC
1 2 3 4 5 6 7 8 9 10   ❖   Newly Illustrated Edition

1 2 3 4 5 6 7 8 9 10

CHILDREN'S ROOM

E SCHERTLE

*To Chad,*
*Dave, and Marie*
—A.S.

*To*
*Kate Newark Pasco*
—T.R.

Tonight a parade marched through Hattie's house.

One was Lumpy, who had been white when he was new. Now he was a nice, comfortable gray.

Two was Dinah, who needed a little help standing up.

**3**

**Four** was Parker, who had lost one ear in the washing machine.

**Three** was Tom, who used to sing "Yankee Doodle" until something inside him went *snap!*

Though he couldn't sing anymore, Tom still looked very smart in a parade.

Five was Hairy. He
was more lovable than
he looked.

**6** Six was Boomer, the big one.

**Seven** had been called Clam Chowder ever since he fell into Hattie's soup.

Eight was Dink, the little one.

Nine was Mabel, who
had come in the mail
on Hattie's birthday.

# 10

Ten was Hattie herself. Hattie was last, or first, or in the middle of the parade, depending on where she was needed. She picked up those who fell over and kept things moving along.

When the parade wound its way into the living room, Mama played the piano and Daddy watched the ten march around and around.

Finally Mama said, "Bedtime, Hattie, my dearie, my dove." Daddy and Mama helped Hattie carry everyone upstairs. Boomer was an armful all by himself.

They put everyone away. Then Daddy pulled back the covers and Hattie jumped in.

Now there was **1** in Hattie's bed.

Mama said, "Good night, Hattie, my dearie, my dove."

"Mama," said Hattie, "Lumpy is cold. He wants to sleep in my bed."

"Lumpy has a big fur coat to keep him warm," said Mama.

"His fur is cold," Hattie told her.

So Mama took Lumpy from the shelf, and then there were **2** in Hattie's bed.

Mama said, "Good night, Hattie, my dearie, my dove."

"I forgot," said Hattie. "Dinah is sick. She'll feel better in my bed."

"Dinah looks fine to me," said Daddy.

"She has inside chicken pox," Hattie told him. "You can't tell by looking."

"I hope it isn't catching," said Daddy. He took Dinah off the dresser, and then there were **3** in Hattie's bed.

Daddy said, "Good night, Hattie, my dearie, my dove."

"Wait," said Hattie. "Tom wants to sleep in my bed. He's afraid of the dark."

"I haven't turned the light out yet," said Mama.

"Tom will make a fuss when you do," Hattie told her.

So Tom came out of the toy box, and then there were **4** in Hattie's bed.

Mama said, "Good night, Hattie, my dearie, my dove."

"Oh, Daddy," said Hattie, "Parker wants to come in, too. If we don't let him, he'll chew the curtains."

"He will?" said Daddy.

"Yes, and the table, too," Hattie told him. "And the carpet."

"We'd better let him in, then," said Daddy.

And so there were **5** in Hattie's bed.

Daddy said, "Good night, Hattie, my dearie, my dove."

"Guess what, Mama," said Hattie. "We have to let Hairy sleep in my bed. I promised him."

"Oh, well, if you promised," said Mama.

And so there were **6** in Hattie's bed.

Mama said, "Good night, Hattie, my dearie, my dove."

"Look, Daddy," said Hattie, "Clam Chowder is uncomfortable in the toy box. When he's uncomfortable, he snores."

"I wonder where he'd be more comfortable," said Daddy.

And soon there were 7 in Hattie's bed.

Daddy said, "Good night, Hattie, my dearie, my dove."

"One more thing," said Hattie. "Boomer's afraid there are chickens in the closet. He wants to sleep with me."

"Hattie," said Mama, "you know perfectly well there are no chickens in the closet."

"I know," said Hattie. "But Boomer thinks there are."

And so there were 8 in Hattie's bed.

Mama said, "Good night, Hattie, my dearie, my dove."

"Daddy?"

"Now what, Hattie?"

"Mabel feels left out, Daddy. She thinks nobody loves her. She might run away."

"We wouldn't want Mabel to do that," said Daddy.

And so there were 9 in Hattie's bed.

Daddy said, "Good night, Hattie, my dearie, my dove."

"What about Dink, Mama?"

"Hattie, there really isn't room for one more."

"Dink is very, very small, Mama."

And then there were **10** in Hattie's bed.

Mama tucked the covers all around. "Good night, Lumpy," she said. "Good night, Dinah. Good night, Tom, Parker, Hairy, Clam Chowder, Boomer, Mabel, and Dink. I really think that's enough, don't you, Hattie?"

" . . . Hattie?"

And then there were **10** in Hattie's bed.

Mama tucked the covers all around. "Good night, Lumpy," she said. "Good night, Dinah. Good night, Tom, Parker, Hairy, Clam Chowder, Boomer, Mabel, and Dink. I really think that's enough, don't you, Hattie?"

" . . . Hattie?"